PANDA-MONIUM
AT
PEEK ZOO

KEVIN
WALDRON

templar books
an imprint of Candlewick Press

A new panda has been born at Peek Zoo!
Mr. Peek the zookeeper and his son, Jimmy,
are busy making her feel at home.

Her name is Lulu and she is a VIP —
a Very Important Panda!

Mr. Peek decides to hold
a **special event**
to celebrate.

The Daily P

NO NEWS IS
GOOD NEWS

**FREE DAY
AT PEEK ZOO**
TO CELEBRATE THE ARRIVAL
OF OUR **NEW BABY PANDA**
SATURDAY, JUNE 23rd
GATES OPEN AT 9 AM SHARP
**DON'T MISS
THE ANIMAL PARADE!**

51 PACES

Mr. Peek daydreams
about the animal parade.

"How heavenly it will be:
animals marching through the zoo
in a perfect straight line—everything
in apple-pie order."

The night before the big day, Mr. Peek prepares a to-do list.

1. Feed giraffes
2. Feed penguins
3. Check gecko tank
4. Check polar bear pool
5. Clean elephants
6. Clean tortoises
7. Feed monkeys
8. Feed pandas

Early the next morning, he steps out proudly
in his bottle-green uniform with Jimmy by his side.

They share the jobs between them.

"Oh, gosh!" says Mr. Peek. "I forgot to include 'Feed the lion' on the list!
But leave that to me. Mr. Whiskerwitz will not be forgotten. Jimmy, my boy,
everything is tickety-boo for our big day at Peek Zoo!"

First Jimmy feeds Angela and Egbert, the two giraffes — though he needs a little help to lock the door.

Meanwhile, Mr. Peek
feeds the penguins —

POOL AREA
KEEP GATE
CLOSED!

but he forgets to shut the gate.

Jimmy checks the temperature in the geckos' tank. Little Harold helps him record the figures in his daily report.

Mr. Peek does the same for the polar bear . . . but he is not really paying attention.

"Let's **cool** the pool down for you, Herbert," he says.

Jimmy washes Eleanor and her baby elephants . . .
and they provide a handy car wash!

Mr. Peek polishes the tortoises,
but he's in a bit of a rush.

"Must hurry, Horace!"
he says. "Lots to do!"

Jimmy knows how to keep the monkeys happy.
He feeds them lots of bananas so they'll be ready
to entertain the crowds.

Mr. Peek feeds the pandas their bamboo, then hurries off to take care of Mr. Whiskerwitz . . . perhaps a little **TOO** quickly.

It's only NOW, as he almost trips over a flapping flipper, that Mr. Peek spots his band of black-and-white followers . . .

though he doesn't notice **all** of them. . . . .

"Dash it!

How did you all get here?"

"Come along, Jimmy!" Mr. Peek calls.
"Help me get these penguins home,
will you? Hurry up, everyone!
Follow me, now. I'm awfully sorry,
Mr. Whiskerwitz. I'll have
to feed you later."

Hippo

Penguins

ars

Lion

oos

But not **everyone** follows Mr. Peek. . . .

On his way back to the penguin pool,
Mr. Peek realizes that all is **not** well.

The tortoises are an unusual color,
poor Herbert is sweating,
and **worse still** . . .

LULU IS MISSING!

"APPLESAUCE!" Mr. Peek cries.
"This is a DISASTER! Where can she be?"

He races all around the zoo, but the panda cub
is nowhere to be seen.

Meanwhile, visitors begin to arrive at the gates.

Mr. Peek arrives back at the penguin pen
just as the zoo clock chimes nine.

"Hurry up!" he says. "In you go!
We've got a panda to find."

There's no way the zoo can open in such a state!
The situation calls for an emergency
Peek Plan of Action.

Jimmy is quick to act.

spruces up the tortoises' shells . . .

He cools Herbert down with plenty of ice . . .

and has everything back in apple-pie order
before you can say hipp-o-pot-a-mus!

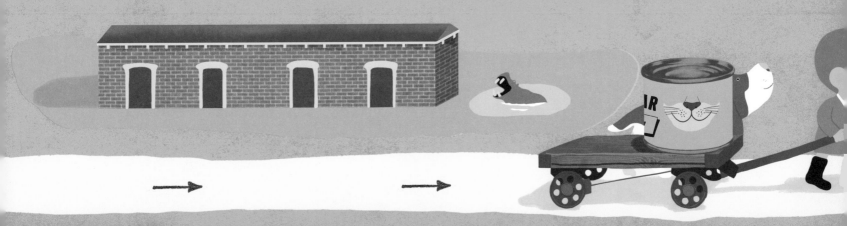

But there is still one thing left for him to do.

At the same time, Mr. Peek braves the waiting public with the Peek Plan of Action **Masterstroke:**

"Welcome to Peek Zoo! We have a special prize today for the first visitor to spot the baby panda!"

He opens the gates . . .

and herds of humans flock into the zoo.

"Goodness!" Mr. Peek yelps.
"You're awfully eager."

A little girl is the first to spot Lulu,
and the crowd gathers around.
But when Mr. Peek scrambles to his feet
to see for himself, he freezes.

"Gadzooks!" he shouts. "Lulu's in the lion's den—and I forgot to feed him!

It's going to be

PANDA-MONIUM!"

But even the really wild beasts are on friendly terms with Jimmy.

"Not to worry, Dad," he says. "I've fed Mr. Whiskerwitz."

ROAR

For hungry lions

It seems there's nothing Mr. Whiskerwitz likes more than a good play . . .

"PHEW!"

and he is as gentle as a lamb with the panda cub.

It's the perfect time to start the big event:

Ladies and Gentlemen
BOYS & GIRLS
PEEK ZOO
PROUDLY PRESENTS
THE EVENT OF A LIFETIME
LET THE
ANIMAL
PARADE
begin
!!!

And Mr. Peek's dream comes true: animals marching in a perfect straight line, everything in apple-pie order, not a **SLIP-UP** in sight. . . .

After a **long day**, father and son take a well-deserved rest.

WET PAINT

"Just as I said, everything is tickety-boo at Peek Zoo!"
sighed Mr. Peek happily.

Well, most of the time, anyway!